Cyberkids 2

W9-CFE-165

The Great Escape

PAUL COLLINS

Illustrated by Peter Foster

Triple3Play

sundance™
A Haights Cross Communications Company

A Haights Cross Communications ®Company

Published by
Sundance Publishing
P.O. Box 740
One Beeman Road
Northborough, MA 01532
800-343-8204

Copyright © text Paul Collins 1999
Copyright © illustrations Peter Foster 1999

First published 1999 as Supa Dazzlers by
Addison Wesley Longman Australia Pty Limited
95 Coventry Street
South Melbourne 3205 Australia
Exclusive United States Distribution: Sundance Publishing

ISBN-13: 978-0-7608-4796-1
ISBN-10: 0-7608-4796-7

Printed in China

Contents

Chapter 1

The Price Of Fame

I was suddenly the most popular kid in town. It was around the neighborhood in five seconds. Don Sousa had knocked out Lee Brookes's fighter in the second round with a virtual gymnast in leotards!

The phone calls started at eight o'clock on the morning after my triumph. By ten o'clock, kids were ringing the doorbell asking me to shoot baskets with them.

Brooksy was looking for me. But word had it that he wouldn't touch me . . . yet, because I was too famous right now. Everyone loved me.

"Watch your back," kids whispered to me. But I felt indestructible. *Nothing* and no one could touch *me!*

Even Teagan Miles phoned to invite me to her party. *Teagan Miles!*

If beating stupid, pig-face Lee Brookes could get me this much fame, imagine how popular I would be if I beat Ming Siou Loong—The Jade Dragon!

But could I "borrow" my sister's virtual gymnast again?

You bet I could!

My victory went to my head. It consumed me.

I told Mom to hold all my calls and to tell everyone I was out if they came to the house. I needed time—time to figure out how I could get Nova's virtual playstation next Saturday night, the very night she needed it for her science project presentation.

Chapter 2

MY Great Challenge

You wouldn't believe how it upset me, having to steal Nova's playstation. It really did. She couldn't stop talking about the big night all day Saturday. Mom gave Nova the money to get a new hairdo. Then they went out, and Nova got to buy a great new outfit for the presentation. And while they were doing all that, I was getting in as much practice with the gymnast as I could. By the time I was finished with her, she was doing full circles in the air with double front-kicks and reverse-punches.

I took Nova's playstation while she was reading an acceptance speech to Mom, just in case she won.

How could I do such a lousy thing to her? I
don't know what got into me. Something
possessed me. It was fame. I'd had a taste of
it all week, and I wanted it full-time. I wanted
everything.

I'd challenged Ming Siou Loong earlier in the
week. By Wednesday, the Dojo had put up
House-Full posters.

There was even a waiting list of kids who wanted to see the fight. Guys like Art Meecham made a bundle of money by selling whole rows of tickets at twice their original price.

I didn't need Duran, although I hired him just in case. If I won tonight, I'd need him to keep the crowds back. In fact, I offered him full-time employment, but he said he was too busy doing other stuff.

Ming Siou Loong didn't look too worried. She didn't even glance at me across the ring. I saw her stretch a couple of times. I'd heard that she had watched a video of my last fight. Well, it wouldn't do her much good.

She could flip her ponytails as much as she wanted.

Ming went through her usual ritual. She spoke a few Chinese words and then bowed her head.

I'd watched her perform that ritual hundreds of times. But this time, Ming's superstitious ritual made me feel a bit nervous. It was like she was calling on an unseen power or something.

To take my mind off her, I punched the start key on my board. The silver-white gymnast grew from the floor up, materializing like an ancient goddess from the canvas.

This time no one laughed. There was an expectant hush. Everyone was straining to see the gymnast in her silver leotards—the fighter who had thrashed Lee Brookes with a second-round knockout.

I smirked a bit and looked over at Ming Siou Loong. She yawned.

The judge announced the rules of kung fu. I had chosen this style because of the gymnast's flexibility and speed. Ming's fighter was agile, but she clocked in much slower than the gymnast.

The gong boomed out. The ref's whistle blew.

Chapter 3

Point scoring

My gymnast somersaulted forward and lashed out with two quick punches. Ming's fighter ducked both, then did a handstand and snap-kicked my gymnast in the chest.

Five points.

I'd never seen Ming's fighter do that before!

I spun the gymnast around and did a reverse side-kick. Missed.

Ming's fighter leaped, led with her right leg, and snapped her left foot into the gymnast's chest.

Ten points.

What was wrong? What was happening
here? This was impossible. Ming's fighter just
couldn't do this stuff!

By the third round, Ming had fifty-eight
points to my thirty-three.

I had to compose myself. I'd stolen from my own sister for this moment. I wasn't going to lose. I had to win, if only to justify my treachery—at least to myself.

The gymnast did a back-flip. Ming's fighter darted forward. But the gymnast slid to one side, lifted her foot high in the air, and did a simple side-kick.

Five points. Ming hadn't expected anything so primitive as a head-high side-kick. I led with the gymnast's left leg, raised it high, and leaped into the air. A perfect front-kick, right square into her opponent's face. *Ten points*!

I didn't dare look at the scoreboard, but it had to be close. Ming's fighter flurry-punched, so the gymnast ducked fast, then spun on the canvas and decked Ming's fighter.

Two points.

The gong sounded.

I pulled my sweaty hands from the control mitts and wiped them dry. My head was buzzing, man. Someone began chanting Ming's name, and then others took it up. Well, I didn't care. I was going to whip her.

The next round began evenly. Ming's fighter did some fancy footwork and knocked the gymnast to the canvas. What surprised Ming, though, was the speed with which the gymnast retaliated. See, my gymnast was smaller than even Ming's fighter. And that meant she needed less power to run.

A reverse-punch, back-knuckle fist, and jumping high-kick combo gave me ten points. I got so carried away in that sixth round that I didn't realize an eerie silence had descended on the Dojo Center.

Everyone should have been screaming right now.

But like I said, I was too consumed to notice.
I was after blood—The Jade Dragon's.

Chapter 4

Dragon Blood!

I didn't even notice the gymnast fading away to nothing. Her power had finally given out. My eyes were glazed, my mind totally focused on my fingers, controlling my gymnast like she was a marionette on strings.

The death buzzer signaled the end of the match just as my gymnast winked out. I blinked the sweat from my eyes. What had

happened? Someone shook me by the shoulder.

"C'mon, kid. It's over." The words were hard-edged. Unfriendly.

It was the judge. I looked over at Ming. Her face was a mess. She looked like she'd been through a wringer or something. Even her warrior ponytails hung limply, like a cocker spaniel's ears. I looked around the Dojo Center.

That's when I felt it—pure hatred. Everyone was glaring at me.

Duran came over. "Congratulations, Don. But look, I've got a date with that cute redhead over there. Your time's almost up. You want me to walk you home?"

Then I looked at the scoreboard.

I blinked twice at the burning LED board.

Ming Siou Loong, ninety-nine points. Don Sousa, one hundred points.

I'd won by one point! But how come no one was cheering me? What was wrong with everyone?

I got up and let Duran guide me down the stairs. My legs were unsteady. Someone booed. Others called me names. A barrage of potato chip bags, soda cans, and all kinds of stuff came flying out of the crowd. Some of it hit the floor. Some hit me. I heard Duran curse and felt his grip on me tighten.

Suddenly Duran pulled me down and out through the turnstiles like I was an escaped convict. I turned to speak to him. "I don't get it!" I yelled. I wanted to go back in there and demand an apology. "They can't do this to me! I'm the *winner!*"

Sweat beaded on Duran's forehead. He pushed me through a blockade of kids who had gathered at the doorway.

Duran saved my life.

When we were out of there and into the dark, cold night, Duran turned to me. "You

still don't get it, do you, Don? You beat the local champion, jerk. No one likes that. Don't you know anything? You were *supposed* to lose."

A girl came running from the entrance. It was Duran's date. They walked me home and left me at my door.

"Be seein' ya, Champ," was all Duran said, as he walked off with his arm around the girl's shoulders.

I felt so miserable I almost cried. I'd cost Nova her chance at the Science Achievement Award. And for what? Everyone hated me. My own family would disown me. I'd be an outcast.

Chapter 5

Dumb Luck

Well, I knew I'd have to face the music sooner or later. So I marched into the house, expecting to be attacked by a crazed Nova.

Instead, Dad came over and offered me a glass of raspberry lemonade. "After deserting your sister tonight, Don, you don't deserve to share in the celebration. You might at least have thought of coming to the presentation ceremony."

Numbly I accepted the glass. "You mean, you won tonight?" I asked Nova.

"Don't look so surprised, Don," she said. She was still flushed from her success. Set out on the floor was her winning project—a virtual city, complete with power-booster rods and moving vehicles. I'd never seen anything like it. How could my dorky sister invent something so cool?

Nova's face suddenly changed. "Hey, what are you doing with my gymnast, Don?" She took it from under my arm.

"I thought the gymnast was your science project," I said slowly.

"Yeah, right," Nova laughed. "That's my workout model for finger control, dummy." She giggled hysterically, and Mom and Dad joined in. "You're a joker, Don. Seriously."

I could have keeled over with relief. Oh, thank you, thank you, I repeated to myself over and over. Then a startling thought came to me. If the gymnast was only a workout model for Nova's fingers, then I'd actually beaten Ming Siou Loong on my own merits. I, Don Sousa, had beaten the queen of the Dojo. By myself, without trickery!

Nah. Who was I kidding? Without the gymnast, I would've gotten trashed.

Then the doorbell rang. I opened the door to . . . Ming Siou Loong.

For a second, I thought she was going to call me a cheat, a fake.

Hesitantly, I said, "Ah, hi."

Ming's smile was strained, but it was there. "Hi. Look, congratulations on your win tonight. Considering you were so far behind on points at one stage, you really made a great comeback. I've never seen an opponent so totally focused."

"Really?" OK, so I was lost for words!

"I'd also like to apologize for the way everyone sort of got angry. I guess it was just the shock of my losing to a rank outsider. You know, no one thought you stood a chance. A gymnast!" She burst out laughing then. "I mean, really, Don. Lee Brookes is still being laughed at. He'll never live it down."

We both cracked up laughing.

After we stopped, Ming hit me with a real whammy. "Say, I had a position in the

National Doubles Championship offered to me a few months back, but I passed it up. I told them I needed to find a really top fighting partner first. Someone who was fast and slick—you know, showy. I found him tonight."

I gulped. "You mean me?"

"No one else," she said.

"Yeah, yeah! When do we start working out?"

"Tomorrow morning, my place." She looked over my shoulder. "I guess I'd better let you get back to your celebrations."

"Oh, that's not for me. My sister won the Science Achievement Award for her virtual city. I didn't bother telling my folks that I'd won tonight. You know, I, ah . . . "

"You what? I don't *believe* this!"

Ming grabbed me by the arm and dragged me into the living room.

"Er, you don't understand, Ming." I struggled to slow her down, but she was determined. "It's not as easy as all that—"

Mom looked up from Nova's neon-bright cityscape. Dad and Nova were polishing off their lemonade. They turned to look at us.

"Join the party," Dad said, and began pouring another glass of raspberry lemonade.

Ming took the glass from Dad and held it up. She looked admiringly at me. "You should make a toast to Don. He won a major virtual fight tonight at the Dojo Center."

I cringed inside. To Ming, the Dojo Center was *the* coolest place in the entire world, and to win there was the ultimate. But to most people, including Mom and Dad, it was a place where punks hung out. They didn't like me going there.

"Ah," Dad said uncertainly. "Well, we have two winners tonight, don't we?"

Nova turned and stared at me.

Oops! Bagged.

Chapter 6

BaggeD

Nova looked at her virtual playstation, then looked back at me. "Don, you didn't actually steal my gymnast and put her through a tacky routine in front of the jerks at the Center, did you?"

I tried smiling, but failed miserably. "I didn't exactly *steal* her, Sis. I *borrowed* her. Look, you have your gymnast back. Just as good as . . . "

"Yeah, but I didn't give you permission—"

"Hold it, guys," Dad said. He looked down at me. "Did Nova, or did she not, give you permission to use her gymnast?"

"Not really, Dad, but—"

"Yes, or no?"

I shook my head.

"I think I'd better go," Ming said. She looked hopefully at my family. "He's a really good virtual fighter. You should be proud of him."

It was the worst thing she could have said at that moment, but somehow I felt proud that she had. The Jade Dragon had paid me a top compliment.

I showed Ming to the door. I leaned forward and gave her a quick kiss on the cheek. I couldn't help it.

Before she could say anything, I shut the door and turned back to my family.

I was in for it now . . .

I was grounded for a week for taking Nova's virtual playstation. I knew Nova let me off lightly. She knew I'd taken it even though I had thought it was her entry into the Science Achievement Awards. If Mom or Dad had realized that, I wouldn't have just been grounded. I would've been buried!

About the Author

Paul Collins

About the only distinguishing feature of Paul Collins's early teacher conferences was that teachers often accused him of daydreaming. He firmly says that everything he is writing now has been thirty-odd years in the making. He would like to meet those teachers again, if only to prove that he wasn't daydreaming at all; rather he was making up stories for when he left school.

About the Illustrator

Peter Foster

Peter Foster was born in 1931 and began to draw at a very early age. When he was just four years old, he got into trouble for drawing a canoe on the living room wall with his sister's lipstick.

In middle school he got into trouble for drawing comic-strip characters in the back of his math book. Finally, his dad found an unending supply of paper for him, and the years following were happily filled with drawing comics.

These days, he illustrates children's books and draws award-winning cartoon strips.